To Charlie – R.B

SPLASH!
by Henrietta Branford and Rosalind Beardshaw
British Library Cataloguing in Publication Data
A catalogue record of this book is available from the British Library.

ISBN 0 340 85550 9 (HB)
ISBN 0 340 85280 1 (PB)

First edition published 2003
10 9 8 7 6 5 4 3

Published by Hodder Children's Books
a division of Hodder Headline Limited
338 Euston Road London NW1 3BH

Printed in China

Splash!

Henrietta Branford
Rosalind Beardshaw

Hodder
Children's
Books

A division of Hodder Headline Limited

Sand in my ears,
Sand in my hair,
Warm sand, wet sand,
Sand EVERYWHERE.

Sand in my belly button,
Tickling my skin.

When I want to wash it off,
I'll JUMP right in.

JUMP into the water,
The icy-spicy water,
   Shivery-shakey water,
         From the deep blue sea.

Deep down under,
What can I see?
A wriggly-squiggly thingummyjig,
As tiny as a flea.

Hidey-glidey scuttlemops,
One, two, three,
And a little pink crab,
Who's hiding from me.

Now JUMP into the water,
The icy-spicy water,
Shivery-shakey water,
From the deep blue sea.

Take a quick dip off a big black rock,
Climb right up to the scaredy-cat top.

Flick
my seaweed tail,
Comb my seaweed hair,

Then slide back down,

As fast as I dare.

And JUMP into the water,
The icy-spicy water,
Shivery-shakey water,
From the deep blue sea.